CH/c

☞ **W9-BPM-081**

Batwings and the Curtain of Night

by Marguerite W. Davol

illustrated by Mary GrandPré

Orchard Books ~ New York

*For Susan, Jonathan, and Sarah — my best creations,
my critics, my champions — M.W. D.*

*For Tom — astronomer, traveling companion, and dream
finder — thank you — M.G.*

Batwings and the Curtain of Night is an original story. It was inspired by a
storyteller's brief tale, the source unknown. As often happens, the
teller heard it from another storyteller, who heard it from another . . .

Text copyright © 1997 by Marguerite W. Davol

Illustrations copyright © 1997 by Mary GrandPré

Orchard Books
95 Madison Avenue
New York, NY 10016

Manufactured in the United States of America
Printed by Barton Press, Inc.   Bound by Horowitz/Rae
Typography design by Chris Hammill Paul

10 9 8 7 6 5 4 3 2 1

The text of this book is set in 15 point Post Mediaeval.   The illustrations are pastel.

Library of Congress Cataloging-in-Publication Data
Davol, Marguerite W.
    Batwings and the curtain of night / by Marguerite W. Davol ;
illustrated by Mary GrandPré.
        p.   cm.
    "A Melanie Kroupa book"–Half t.p.
    Summary: After creating the world and its creatures and day and
night, the Mother of All Things leaves it to the night animals to find a
way to lessen the night's darkness.
    ISBN 0-531-30005-6.–ISBN 0-531-33005-2 (lib. bdg.)
    [1. Creation – Fiction. 2. Animals – Fiction. 3. Night – Fiction.]
I. GrandPré, Mary, ill.   II. Title.
PZ7.D32155Bat   1997
[E]–dc20   96-42482

Batwings and the Curtain of Night

A Melanie Kroupa Book

Back when the world first began, there was no day, no night. The Mother of All Things stood where the four corners of the world meet and looked in every direction.

She saw the land and water, the deserts and swamps, the hills and plains. She saw the mountains and, arching over all the earth, the sky.

"The world is wide," she said, "but dull and gray. It needs light, bright light."

Digging deep within the earth, the Mother of All Things brought out a lump of clay. She molded it into a perfect ball, then tossed it up, high into the sky. As it rose, the spinning ball began to glow, brighter, brighter, bringing light and warmth throughout the world. And day was born.

"Now the world is beautiful," she said, "but empty." She reached down into the pocket of her ample skirts and brought out a handful of seeds. These she scattered far and wide upon the earth. Flowers and ferns, grasses and trees began to grow, covering the land.

Still the Mother of All Things was not satisfied. Earth needed something more. She gathered up her ample skirts, then shook them. Creatures large and small—elephants and ants, eagles, snakes, and snails—tumbled out to settle land and sea.

Her finger touched the birds that stirred the air and each animal that ran or crawled across the land. She gathered in her hands the fish swimming in the sea and let them go. And with her touch, each creature was given its place upon the earth.

The Mother of All Things rejoiced as plants grew and animals multiplied. Color filled the world. But she soon saw that all the brilliant sunlight needed tempering. Plants and animals needed rest.

Gathering dark fronds of ferns and branches of fir trees, the Mother of All Things began to weave a curtain, dark and thick, a curtain that she stretched across the sky. And night was born.

The animals, large and small alike, were happy under the curtain of night. Now they could close their eyes against the brilliant sun. Now they could sleep.

But the Mother of All Things saw that the long
hours of dark were much too barren and silent,
so she reached into her wide sleeves and pulled forth
animals that thrive at night—the owl and
sloth, the panther and coyote. The bat.

Then she was satisfied. "I leave you now," she said. "The world is in your care." With that, the Mother of All Things disappeared beyond the sky.

Earth's creatures were content. Each dawn the mourning dove greeted the sun as the curtain of night rolled back. Each dusk the plaintive thrush bade the ball of sun good-bye as the curtain of night unrolled and stretched out across the sky.

After night had followed day more times than can be counted, however, the animals and birds that prowl and hunt under cover of darkness grew more and more discontented. One night they gathered where the sand meets the sea and began to complain loudly.

"Night is too dark," the owl hooted. "I bump into branches."

"My prey gets away," the panther snarled. "I'm hungry!"

"It's too dark to run," the coyote whined. "I stub my toes on logs. And howl!"

"But the sun is too bright," the sloth drawled, "and sometimes wakes me up."

"The sun makes my head ache," the owl added, "and I can't think!"

With grunts and growls, hoots and howls, the night creatures voiced their complaints. All agreed—although it was much too dark, they preferred the night. Day was too bright. They must change the night—but how? Each animal had a different idea and argued loudly about what to do.

From far beyond the curtain of night, the Mother of All Things heard the creatures' noisy grumbling. With a wave of her hand, a wind of silence swirled over the world. "Find a way," she whispered. "You must find a way."

In the silence the owl closed her wise eyes and thought for a long time. Finally she spoke. "One of us must pull aside the curtain of night. We must let in a little light."

The creatures looked up. Pull back the wide curtain of night? Too far away. Too hard. Who is strong enough? "Not I," each said. "Impossible, not I!"

Finally the bat wriggled his sharp claws and squeaked, "I'm not strong, true, but if all the bats in the world fly up and together we grab the curtain of night, maybe we can pull it back a little."

The owl nodded. "You must try."

The word went out. Bats from everywhere gathered as the curtain of night unrolled across the sky. In one enormous swoop and swirl, black clouds of bats headed up into the sky. But the way was long, too long, and the distance far, too far. One by one the bats fell back to earth, exhausted, their wings limp. "The sky is too high," they squeaked.

Then the coyote had an idea. "Cling to my back and I'll run up the highest hill. From there you can reach the sky."

Bats settled onto the coyote. Indeed, from the hilltop they flew higher than before, but not high enough.

Next the sloth said, "Cling to me and I'll climb the tallest tree on the hill. Then you can reach the sky."

Bats piled onto the sloth's back. Very slowly they inched up the tree. Indeed, from the treetop the bats flew even higher, but not high enough.

Stretching his long night-black shape, the panther said,
"Now it is my turn. Cling to my back and I'll search out
the highest mountain. Surely from its top you can reach
the sky."

"I'll join you," said the owl. "My wings are wide, my
talons large."

Bats crowded onto the panther's back and the owl
perched on his head. Together they climbed the highest
mountain. When they reached the peak, they looked up.
The sky, almost dark by now, still seemed very far away.
Could they reach it?

The owl said, "We must all fly as high as our hearts
will allow."

With a mighty whirl, the bats and the
owl soared toward the sky. Struggling
upward, they flew and flew until they
thought their hearts would burst. But no
one gave up.

This time they reached
the curtain of night. Every
bat grabbed with its claws.
Hanging upside down, they
pulled and pulled together. Owl, too, dug in her
great talons. She yanked and tugged. But the
curtain of night did not budge. One by one
the bats fluttered wearily to earth, their
wings tattered. Finally the owl, too, glided
down, defeated. They had failed.

But when the creatures looked up, they were astonished. The dark was not so dark! Wherever the bats' sharp claws had clung, a glitter of light appeared. And where the owl's talons had tugged, a large hole let the light shine through.

The Mother of All Things looked out at the night creatures below. She nodded, pleased.

"Owl, now you can see to fly, and coyote can run," she said. "Panther, you can see to hunt, and sloth . . ." But sloth was stretched out, fast asleep.

To this day all creatures that prefer the night welcome the light from the moon and stars to guide them through the dark. And to this day colonies of bats crowd together and cling upside down.